Michaela Morgan has written over a hundred books for children.
She has been shortlisted for the Children's Book Award,
been an International Reading Association Children's Choice
and won a United Kingdom Reading Association award.
Her other book for Frances Lincoln is *Night Flight*.

Michelle Cartlidge was born in London and now lives in Mousehole, Cornwall.
She became a student at both Hornsey College of Art and the Royal College of Art.
Her first book, *Pippen and Pol* won the Mother Goose Award.
Her Teddy Trucks books were made into a BBC TV cartoon series.

Brave Mouse is featured on ITV's Signed Stories website (www.signedstories.com),
which makes picture books accessible for deaf children.

For brave mice everywhere

First published in Great Britain in 2004 by
Frances Lincoln Children's Books, 4 Torriano Mews, Torriano Avenue, London NW5 2RZ

First paperback published in Great Britain and in the USA in 2010

www.franceslincoln.com

A catalogue record for this book is available from the British Library.

ISBN 978-1-84780-110-4

Set in ITC Stone Sans and Kidprint

Printed in Jurong Town, Singapore by Star Standard Industries in December 2009

1 3 5 7 9 8 6 4 2

BRAVE
Mouse

Michaela Morgan
and Michelle Cartlidge

F

FRANCES LINCOLN
CHILDREN'S BOOKS

Little Mouse was scared of all sorts of things.

Dark shadows scared him.

Bright lights scared him.

Loud noises scared him.

And silence scared him too.

One day Mum and Dad said, "We're going out for a while. The babysitter will look after you until we get back."

Little Mouse did not
like this one bit.
His ears began to droop.

His whiskers
began to twitch.

A big tear started
to run down his nose.

Then a little voice inside him said,

They'll be back soon. Wait and see.
You're a brave mouse – as brave as brave can be!

And Little Mouse took a deep breath
and waved bye-bye.

And later they DID come back and they hugged him and they loved him and they stroked his little ears.

"What a big brave mouse you are!" said Mum.

The first time Little Mouse went to the swimming pool, he didn't like it one bit.

He stood and he shivered.

His ears drooped.

His whiskers quivered.

The water looked cold and deep.
It smelled funny and everything was so LOUD.

Then a little voice inside him said,

Perk up your whiskers. Dip in a toe.
You're a brave, brave mouse, so have a go!

And Little Mouse did have a go. And he loved it!

He splished

and he **splashed**

and he **sploshed**

until it was time
to go home.

Little Mouse did all sorts of brave things.

Go on, try a bit. Take a little bite.
You're a brave, brave mouse. It might taste all right!

You're a brave, brave mouse – open wide.
Let the dentist peek inside.

It's only a shadow in the night.
If you reach out, you can switch on the light.

One day Little Mouse went to the playground.
There was a big shiny slide, a wibbly-wobbly
bridge, and a bouncing duck.
The children shouted to Little Mouse…

"Swing high
like me!"

"Slide fast
like me!"

But Little Mouse didn't really want to climb high
or slide fast.

Then the little voice inside him said,

Are you going to have a go?
You ARE a brave, brave mouse,
you know.

And Brave Mouse said...

"No!"

Brave Mouse stood up tall and bravely,
very bravely made up his own mind.

"It's the bouncing duck
for me!" he said.

Brave Mouse played happily, and as he played,
he sang a little song...

Sometimes I do,
sometimes I don't.
Sometimes I try new things,
sometimes I won't.
I can be brave, the bravest of all.
I can brush my whiskers and stand up tall.
I can speak up, I can squeak up,
so look at me.
I am Brave Mouse.
Brave Mouse, that's me!

MORE BOOKS FROM FRANCES LINCOLN CHILDREN'S BOOKS

Once upon a Time
Niki Daly

Sarie doesn't like school. Every time she has to take out her reading book, her voice disappears and the other children tease her. But one person understands how she feels – Ou Missus, an old lady living across the veld, who tells wonderful stories.

I Have Feelings!
Jana Novotny Hunter
Illustrated by Sue Porter

Everybody has feelings – especially me and you!
"Waking up is my best time – then I'm feeling happy. And when we go to the park I feel really excited. But when my baby sister gets first turn on the swing, I start feeling jealous!" Small children will fall in love with the adorable star of *I Have Feelings!* – an essential book for learning to express how you feel.

See You Later Mum!
Jennifer Northway

William is very excited about his first day of nursery school, but everything is so noisy, he sticks close to Mum. Then he notices someone else who is too shy to join in.

Frances Lincoln titles are available from all good bookshops.
You can also buy books and find out more about your favourite titles,
authors and illustrators on our website: www.franceslincoln.com